DUEL IN THE SKY

Tom and Tony Bradman

Illustrated by John McCrea

EDGE FRANKLIN WATTS

LONDON•SYDNEY

First published in 2014
by Franklin Watts

Cover design by Peter Scoulding

Franklin Watts
338 Euston Road
London NW1 3BH

Franklin Watts Australia
Level 17/207 Kent Street
Sydney, NSW 2000

A CIP catalogue record for this book
is available from the British Library.

(pb) ISBN: 978 1 4451 2381 3
(ebook) ISBN: 978 1 4451 2383 7
(Library ebook) ISBN: 978 1 4451 2385 1

1 3 5 7 9 10 8 6 4 2

Printed in Great Britain by CPI Group (UK) Ltd, Croydon, CR0 4YY

Franklin Watts is a division of Hachette Children's Books,
an Hachette UK company.
www.hachette.co.uk

Contents

Chapter One	Dashing Pilots	4
Chapter Two	Gun Flashes	12
Chapter Three	Into Battle	18
Chapter Four	Surprise Answer	26
Chapter Five	Dogfight Days	32
Chapter Six	No Mercy	39
Chapter Seven	The Hawk	44
Chapter Eight	Fierce Joy	53

Chapter One
Dashing Pilots

The autumn sun had almost dipped under the horizon when George finally spotted the aerodrome. He was flying low, at two hundred feet, the neat French countryside flashing past beneath the wings of his Sopwith Camel biplane, and he gently pushed the joystick forward to begin his descent. Landings always made him nervous, but he managed well enough, the Camel's wheels only bouncing once on the runway.

George eased off the throttle and taxied towards the three hangars, all of which had their doors wide open. He brought his plane to a halt in front of the middle one, glimpsing more Camels in its huge interior. A group of men was waiting, ground crew by the look of them. But there was an officer too, a tall major wearing the distinctive Royal Flying Corps tunic that buttoned down the right-hand side.

George removed his goggles and climbed out of the cockpit with his kitbag, as the ground crew surrounded his plane. He walked over to the officer and saluted. “Lieutenant George Williams reporting for duty, sir,” he said.

“Welcome to the squadron, Williams,” said the officer. “I’m Major Bryant. No need to salute from now on – we don’t much stand on ceremony here. Come along, I’ll take you to the mess so you can meet some of the other chaps and get settled in.”

The Major strode off and George

Lieutenant George Williams reporting for duty, sir.

followed, half running to keep up. Beyond the hangars was a wooden hut with several cars and motorbikes parked outside.

"Tell me about yourself, Williams. Needless to say HQ haven't sent me any info on you."

"There's not much to tell, sir," said George, slightly out of breath. "I was keen to do my bit, of course, and I'd always liked the idea of flying, so I applied to the RFC..."

George had been fascinated by what he'd read in the newspapers about the exploits of the Royal Flying Corps over the Western Front. He'd been particularly thrilled by the stories of the "aces", the dashing pilots who fought aerial duels with their German counterparts. It all seemed far more noble and heroic than the rest of the war, the stalemate in northern France and Flanders, the mud and blood of the trenches.

"That shows you've got brains, at least. How much flying have you done?"

"Thirty-five hours solo so far, sir," George said proudly. "Ten in Camels."

The Major turned to look at him, his eyes narrowed. "Is that all?" George nodded. "Done any fighting?" George hesitated, then shook his head. "How old are you?"

"Eighteen, sir," said George. "I joined up when I was still in the sixth form."

"Good grief," sighed the Major. "I hope the top brass know what they're doing. At this rate they'll be sending me pilots in short trousers. Well, it can't be helped, I suppose. What have you heard about the squadron? Good things, I hope?"

"Oh yes, sir," said George, nodding eagerly. "Very good indeed."

In fact the Major's squadron had the best fighting record in the whole RFC, which was mostly down to the success of a certain Captain David Pembroke. George had followed Pembroke's career, deeply impressed by his tally of confirmed kills. So he had gone out of his way to secure a posting to the great ace's squadron. He couldn't wait to meet Pembroke, to learn from the man himself how to become an ace.

"Here we are," the Major said when they reached the hut. He pushed open the door and ushered George over the threshold, into a dimly lit room that smelt of cabbage and beer and stale cigarette smoke. Faces loomed out of the darkness, eyes staring.

"Well, what do we have here?" said a voice. "Fresh meat for the mincer?"

It seemed that David Pembroke was unimpressed with the new pilot.

Chapter Two
Gun Flashes

There had been several pictures of Pembroke in the papers, so George recognised him at once. The famous ace was sprawled on a sofa in the far corner of the hut, a striking figure with dark hair brushed back from his forehead and a face that was all hard edges, like an eagle's. He was restless like a bird too, one foot tapping away on the floor, his jaw twitching, his eyes fixed on George, who felt himself blushing.

"That will do, Pembroke," the Major snapped, frowning. "You know my feelings about that kind of talk. Anyway, Williams, let me introduce you to everyone..."

Half the squadron was crowded into the small hut, twenty-five young men. Most of the pilots were older than George, but not by much. It was a friendly evening, although George found it hard to relax. Pembroke's remark had been a shock, a setback before George had even got to know the man.

He glanced at the ace from time to time, wondering if he might attempt to recover from such a bad start by speaking to him. But Pembroke seemed unapproachable, the others leaving a space around him as if he were a dangerous wild animal.

"Someone will show you to your billet, Williams," the Major said after a while. "Make sure you get a good night's sleep. Briefing will be at 0600 tomorrow."

A ground-crew sergeant took George to his billet, a nearby farmhouse. It was dark now, but the eastern sky was lit by gun-flashes, and George realised the front was very close, only a few miles away. His room was tiny and he lay on the bed listening to the distant rumble of artillery, trying to obey the Major's order. But it seemed that no sooner had he drifted off to sleep at last than the sergeant was waking him up.

Breakfast was in the mess, bully beef sandwiches and mugs of scalding hot tea from an urn. George's stomach churned with nerves and he couldn't face either, although everyone else seemed fine, the hut full of chatter and laughter. He tried to catch Pembroke's eye but the ace was clearly avoiding him. George was even more puzzled now, wondering why Pembroke was behaving in such a way. It was as if he had decided to dislike him on sight... The Major came in and a tense silence fell.

"Morning, chaps," he said. "Business as usual today. Flight A will take the dawn patrol, and that will include Williams, our new boy..." George blushed again, his nerves instantly increasing – Pembroke was leader of Flight A. He glanced at the ace, who met his gaze with a frown before looking away. "Now don't take any risks, Williams," the Major was saying.

"Stay in formation, watch – and learn..."

It seemed like excellent advice, especially as George had been planning to do that anyway. The Major carried on, assigning the other four Flights to patrols later in the day, giving a run-down of overnight activity in the line. Then it was time to head for the hangars. The ground crew had got the Camels ready – the ten planes of Flight A were standing at one end of the runway, the dawn light glinting off their wings.

George pulled on his flying helmet and goggles and climbed into his plane. A ground-crew private grabbed one tip of his propeller and swung it down hard, the engine instantly sparking into

life. Soon George was taxiing, his eyes on the planes in front, each of them taking off with the roar of engines being given full throttle.

Moments later he was airborne too and flying eastwards — towards the enemy.

Chapter Three
Into Battle

Pembroke's plane was in the lead of course, and he quickly took them up to five thousand feet. There they assumed a tight "v" formation, George filling the position on the extreme right. The sun was properly above the horizon now, the immense sky pale blue and free of clouds. George soon felt the cold biting into his cheeks, and was glad of his gloves and his thick leather flying jacket with its sheepskin lining.

Yet nothing could beat the experience of flying, however cold it might get. Every time George flew there came a moment when he grinned at the thought that he was actually

up in the air, the realm of birds. It seemed completely crazy that this fragile structure of wood and canvas and metal could carry him through the heavens. But the fact that it did was always enormously, unbelievably thrilling.

A sudden chatter of machine-gun fire made George's heart leap. He looked round wildly, thinking they must be under attack. Then he saw that each pilot was firing a test burst to make sure his guns were working. George did the same, thumbing the trigger on his joystick. The two Vickers machine guns under the cowling in front of him – the "hump" that gave the Camel its name – barked satisfyingly in response.

RATA-TAT
RATA-TAT

RATA-TAT
RATA-TAT

To his relief, everything so far had been as he had expected from his training. After a while Pembroke pointed downwards. They had reached the front line, and George stared at it in horrified fascination. The trenches were like great scars on the world, running north and south as far as he could see. Between them was the giant, crater-filled wound of no-man's land. He was flying too high to pick out any troops, but there were plenty of flashes and puffs of smoke from artillery on both sides.

George looked round and saw Pembroke pointing north, his gloved finger jabbing in the direction of some black dots in the sky over enemy territory. For a brief instant George thought they were ravens. Then he realised they were German planes, not birds – and he felt a thrill of pure fear flood through him. Pembroke banked his plane towards them and the rest of Flight A turned to follow him – into battle.

From that moment everything happened at incredible speed. The Germans came at Flight A head on, George recognising the aircraft as Fokker DR1 triplanes. There were at least a dozen, maybe more, each one a different colour – blue, green, red, even yellow. They started firing at the British from a long way out, angry white flashes appearing on their noses, bright showers of tracer bullets filling the sky.

Flight A returned fire until both groups of planes met and lost formation. Pembroke suddenly pulled up in a steep climb, distracting George. Where was the ace going? Should he climb too? A Fokker flashed past barely a few feet in front of George's propeller, sending him into a total panic. He hastily thumbed his trigger, his heart thumping, but the Jerry plane was already long gone and the burst wasted.

All around him planes swooped and dived and fired at each other. George twisted round in his cockpit, trying to find a target and keep control of his Camel at the same time, convinced he was going to die in the next few seconds.

BUD-DA-BUDA
BUD-DA-BUDA
BOOM!

Chapter Four
Surprise Answer

It was over even more quickly than it had begun. One moment George felt as if he were in the centre of chaos, a tangle of roaring planes and chattering machine guns and smoke and flame, and the next he was flying through empty sky. The Jerry planes had broken off the fight and were heading back in the direction they had come, as was the rest of Flight A. George breathed a sigh of relief and followed them.

He was the last to land, and taxied to the hangars. As he climbed out of his plane he saw a line of bullet holes in the fuselage that ended inches from the cockpit. George swallowed, his stomach churning – he didn't remember his plane being hit, but he had clearly had a narrow escape. If the German who had shot up his plane had kept his thumb on the trigger a second longer then he would definitely be dead.

"Are you all right, Williams?" said a voice, startling him. George turned – he hadn't heard the Major approaching. "It seems you've had something of a baptism of fire."

"Yes, sir, quite all right," said George, pulling himself together. "I hope I can do a little better next time. Pembroke brought one of the blighters down, though."

"He got two, actually. But you'll hear about his exploits at the debrief."

"I was wondering, sir... Do you think Pembroke might give me some pointers? On fighting, I mean. I would ask him, but, well...he doesn't seem to like me..."

The Major snorted. "He doesn't much like anybody, I'm afraid, and to be perfectly honest I doubt you'll get any sense out of him. The truth is that he's something of a law unto himself. You'd be a damn sight better off talking to me and the others."

"Thank you, sir, I'll bear that in mind," said George. Of course the Major and the other pilots could probably give him all sorts of useful information. But only Pembroke could tell him what he really wanted to know – how to be an ace. There had to be a way of getting through to him. After all, they were supposed to be on the same side, weren't they? So perhaps it was simply a case of being persistent...

The debrief took place in the mess later that morning. Pembroke reported in a clipped voice what had happened on the patrol – two enemy planes downed for the loss of one of their own. George felt a pang of guilt when he realised he had forgotten that, but it soon passed. The pilot had managed to land his plane in a field behind the British trenches and had survived. Both Jerry pilots had been killed, though.

"Congratulations, Pembroke," said the Major. "How many kills is that now?"

George knew exactly, of course. He looked up at Pembroke standing in front of them and expected him to say "twenty-eight". But Pembroke's answer was a surprise.

"More than enough," he muttered, scowling. Then he stalked out.

There was a lot of tutting and eye-rolling from the others. The Major frowned, then sighed and declared the

debrief completed. George jumped up and hurried after Pembroke, deciding there was no time like the present. Luckily Pembroke hadn't got very far. He was just outside the mess, sitting astride one of the motorbikes.

"Er... I say, Pembroke," George began. "Do you think I could ask..."

Pembroke glanced at him with a strange expression on his face, and opened his mouth as if he were about to speak. Then he shut it and quickly turned away. He kick-started the motorbike, revved the engine till it roared, and shot off at terrific speed.

George watched him go, coughing in the acrid cloud of the exhaust smoke, disturbed by the look of pity he was sure he had seen in Pembroke's eyes.

Chapter Five
Dogfight Days

The next few days were full of patrols. On several occasions George was sent out to spot targets in the Jerry trenches for the artillery, taking photographs with a large camera screwed to the side of his cockpit. It was hard enough doing that and flying at the same time, but there was also the German anti-aircraft fire to deal with. Huge explosions in the sky around him rocked his Camel, spattering it with shrapnel.

There were more battles with Jerry fighters too, or dogfights as George soon learned from the other pilots to call them. It was the right word for the

confusing, terrifying clashes – planes chasing and being chased in their turn, engines snarling, tracers cutting through the sky. Yet even in the middle of all the chaos, George still found the romance, the adventure. When a German pilot saluted him before escaping, he couldn't help but picture himself as a young knight on horseback, returning the salute after a joust. There could be nobility here – honour amongst the terror.

Several pilots in the squadron's other flights were killed – on one particularly bad day, three men in Flight D. There were reports of a deadly new Jerry ace as well, the Hawk – so called because he flew a distinctive black Fokker DR1. Though to his surprise George didn't feel half as scared as he had been to begin with. Of course he had moments of fear in the dogfights, but they passed as quickly as they came.

It was partly a question of getting used to things, knowing what to expect, but the Major and the other pilots helped as well. They told him to get plenty of height and make sure nobody hung on his tail, to watch out for planes coming out of the sun, to fire short bursts from up close and a plane's length ahead of his target. It all seemed sensible, practical advice – but after several weeks he had still barely hit an enemy.

Pembroke was as elusive as ever, both in battle and afterwards. He kept up his tally of kills, downing

German fighters regularly. But no matter how hard George tried to see what Pembroke did so he could work out his tactics, it was impossible. Pembroke always seemed to appear out of nowhere and blast the enemy to smithereens. There was no talking to him either, and George was beginning to think he might never learn how to be an ace.

Late one afternoon, as a fiery sun was setting in the west, George headed to the hangars alone. He wanted a word with the ground crew about the guns on his Camel. They had jammed a couple of times at crucial moments in dogfights, refusing to fire at all and leaving him feeling horribly like a sitting duck. He needed to be certain they wouldn't let him down in future – it really might be a matter of life or death.

George entered the middle hangar and saw Pembroke coming towards him.

"Hello, Pembroke–"

Pembroke held up a hand to silence him and sighed. "It's not going to work, you know. I don't have anything to say

to you. Nothing you'll want to hear, anyway."

"Oh, I doubt that," said George, suddenly determined not to be intimidated. "There's so much you could teach me about everything. I mean...how do you do it?"

"Ah, so it's the secret you're after, is it?" Pembroke was smiling now. "The secret to becoming an ace and getting your name and face in all the newspapers?"

George shrugged and nodded, but he didn't like the way this was going. He felt Pembroke was mocking him, talking to him as if he were a stupid child.

"It's easy," said Pembroke. "You just have to learn to be a ruthless killer."

Chapter Six
No Mercy

George stared at him for a moment, waiting for him to say something else. Beyond them a ground-crew mechanic dropped a spanner on the concrete floor with a clang. Pembroke's eyes were fixed on George's, but he remained irritatingly silent.

"Is that it?" said George. "Surely it's obvious we're here to kill the enemy."

"You weren't listening, were you?" Pembroke snapped. "I said you have to be a ruthless killer. I know why boys like you want to join the RFC. You've read in the papers about duels in the sky and pilots being chivalrous. Well, it's all utter rot. The only way to become an ace is to be absolutely ruthless. You have to be brutal and cunning to get kills – dive on Jerry out of a cloud, sneak up on him from beneath, watch out for the one who's used up his ammo or who's been hit already. An ace has no pity, no mercy, no interest in doing anything but adding to his damned tally."

Pembroke had been speaking with a hushed, quiet intensity and stopped abruptly to catch his breath. He looked out towards the sunset, the side of his jaw twitching.

"I... I don't believe it," George said. "It doesn't have to be like that. I've seen enough now to know it's hard, but we can do what we have to without losing our...our..."

George paused, trying to work out what he meant and find the right word to express it. Pembroke turned to look at him once more. “Our honour?” he said. “There’s nothing honourable about shooting young men like ourselves out of the sky. Have you thought about that?”

“Actually, the word I was thinking of was ... humanity,” said George.

“Then you’re even more of a hopeless case than I thought,” said Pembroke. His voice was full of bitterness, but that look of pity had returned to his eyes. “There can’t be any humanity in war, and especially not in this one. It’s an endless slaughter, in the air as much as in the trenches.”

They fell silent for a while, George

struggling with what Pembroke had said. It went against everything he had grown up with, all the ideas of duty and patriotism and honour in battle that he had been taught at school and on the sporting field. But Pembroke was a warrior, a man who commanded respect for what he had done, and George couldn't bring himself to simply dismiss his words. The more he thought about it – and especially the part about being ruthless – the more it made sense.

"So do you have any advice for me at all?" George said eventually. "You paint a pretty bleak picture, Pembroke. But I can't just turn around and run away."

"No, you're right," Pembroke said quietly, his voice almost a whisper.

"None of us can. What else could someone like me do now anyway? There isn't much to look forward to but more killing, and death, I suppose..." He squared his shoulders and held George's gaze. "Actually, I might have a couple of bits of advice for you, old chap. The first is simple – do whatever you can to survive. Nothing else matters."

"Fine, I'll try," said George, shrugging. "So what's the second one?"

"Even simpler." Pembroke smiled at him properly. "Don't be like me."

Then he walked off, vanishing into the evening's deepening gloom.

Chapter Seven
The Hawk

Two days later George was standing by the hangars with the Major and several other pilots, including Pembroke. Flight B had gone out on the dawn patrol and

was long overdue. Then they saw it, a ragged line of Camels straggling in from the east. The planes landed one after the other, and it was clear that most of them had been badly shot up. George was shocked when he counted them – there were only six.

Almost the entire squadron squeezed into the mess hut for the debrief. They sat silently, listening to the leader of Flight B as he explained what had happened. It seemed that a dozen German planes had come out of nowhere, led by the Hawk in his distinctive black Fokker DR1. He had bagged three Camels himself in quick succession, pursuing one to ground level before finishing it off, the British plane crashing in a ball of fire. Not a single German plane had been shot down.

"Are we sure it was the Hawk?" asked Pembroke. George glanced at him and saw he was leaning forward on his sofa, a look of intense concentration on his face.

"I don't think there can be any doubt," the Major said quietly. "There's also no doubt that we have to hit back as soon as possible – we can't let Jerry get away with this kind of thing. So as of this morning we will be doubling the number of patrols..."

An hour later George took off in his Camel at the rear of Flight A. They climbed to five thousand feet but didn't follow any of their usual patrol routes. Pembroke led them due east

and they soon flew over the line into enemy territory. Visibility was poor, the sky just above them crowded with heavy grey clouds, although George could see the puffs of white smoke from the German anti-aircraft guns below.

He was still worried about his guns. A ground-crew sergeant had checked them and said they were fine. But he had also said all guns jammed sometimes, and showed George how to un-jam them by pulling the bolt back to clear the breech. He did it now, and fired a test burst, both guns behaving as they should, so he relaxed, although only a little. The cold was biting, the wind cutting into his cheeks like a knife.

They flew on, George scanning the horizon for the black dots of enemy planes. He remembered what Pembroke had said about aces sneaking up on their targets from below or behind, and he nervously craned round, checking in every direction. But there were no Jerry fighters in sight, only the German-occupied French countryside rolling underneath his wings, a patchwork of fields and forests, roads and rivers.

Suddenly George glimpsed something, a dark shape bursting out of a thick cloud a few hundred feet above him and to his right. He was startled, then felt a wave of pure fear as the dark shape resolved itself into the unmistakable silhouette of a black

Fokker DR1. The Hawk swooped down on Flight A like a giant bird of prey, firing his guns, two lines of tracers streaming out and raking across the nearest British plane. More German fighters dropped out of the cloud behind him, their guns blazing too.

Flight A broke formation, the Camels turning in different directions, some diving, some climbing, none of them firing back. George flew on in a straight line, unsure what else to do, the sky around him full of tracers and chunks of planes and smoke and fire, all the familiar chaos of a dogfight. Then he felt his Camel judder and he knew he was being hit by a long burst. He closed his eyes, expecting the German machine-gun bullets to rip through his body, but then the juddering stopped. He opened his eyes and glanced over his shoulder, and what he saw terrified him.

Two Jerry fighters were on his tail – and one of them was the Hawk.

Chapter Eight
Fierce Joy

George looked away and concentrated on flying, some instinct telling him to bank steeply to the left, which was just as well. Both German planes started firing at him again, filling the air his Camel had just left with tracer fire, four streams of bullets crossing. He knew there was no point in climbing to get away – that would slow him down. His only chance was to dive, and soon he was plunging through the sky.

The Germans followed him, but at least he had gained some distance and their bursts were falling well short. George pushed the joystick further forward to deepen the dive, and the

Camel began to shake. There was only so much strain the plane could take – he would have to pull out of the dive before the wings were torn off. But if he did it too soon his pursuers would catch up and blow him to pieces anyway.

They were right behind him now, the ground rushing up to meet all three of them, George finally pulling the joystick back hard at less than a hundred feet and throwing the Camel to the right this time. He roared over a wood, his right wingtips narrowly missing the tops of the trees, and swung round in the tightest turn he could manage. Then he levelled off, glanced round – and saw that he had got in behind both German planes!

Mein gott!
RATA-TAT
RATA-TAT

RATA-TAT
RATA-TAT

George's guns barked, the tracers smacking into the tail and fuselage of the Hawk's companion. The German plane slipped onto its side and began to fall from the sky, thick, black smoke pouring from its rear. George kept his thumb on the trigger, a fierce joy flooding through him.

Then two things happened – his guns jammed, and the Hawk turned into the cloud of smoke, vanishing like a ghost in daylight.

George cursed and grabbed the bolt to clear the breech, but it was stuck. He pulled it once, twice, without budging it at all. Then he looked up – and his blood almost froze in his veins. the Hawk had reappeared and was coming at him head on. There would be no time to get out of his way, not by climbing or diving or turning to either side. George knew his only hope was to un-jam his guns and get a burst in first.

"Come on, damn you..." he muttered, trying the bolt again, still with no luck. The gap between him and the Hawk grew smaller and smaller, and George had almost resigned himself to death when another plane flew up beside him, close enough for him to see the pilot was Pembroke. For a few heartbeats they flew together, their eyes locked on each other. Then Pembroke saluted him and dived into the Hawk's path.

The German started firing at that moment, his burst slamming into Pembroke's Camel, the plane

juddering. Chunks of wing and fuselage flew off, but George knew Pembroke had given him the time for one last attempt to un-jam his guns. He yanked on the bolt and it moved just as Pembroke's Camel exploded in a fiery ball. George flew through the flames, thumbing his trigger, praying his guns would fire.

They did; George's burst shattered the Hawk's propeller. The Fokker spun out of control and plunged into the ground, blowing up with a dull boom on impact. George banked to the right and flew back, going as low as he dared, searching for Pembroke's plane. He found the crash site on the other side of the wood, a heap of broken wings and orange fire and more black smoke.

BBZZTTTT!
RATA-TAT
RATA-TAT

No one could have survived that, not even a man such as Pembroke. George circled, thinking it could have been him down there, of how Pembroke had given his own life to save a comrade... Now he saluted the ace, and swore silently that his name would never be forgotten.

Then George turned and flew away, into the blood-red rays of the setting sun.

There are four books to collect!